ONLINE

THE ICE FACTOR

By Jennifer Gray and Amanda Swift

GUINEA PIGS ONLINE

THE ICE FACTOR

JENNIFER GRAY &
AMANDA SWIFT

ILLUSTRATIONS BY
SARAH HORNE

Quercus

First published in Great Britain in 2014 by

Quercus Editions Ltd
55 Baker Street
7th Floor, South Block
London
W1U 8EW

A CIP catalogue reference for this book is available
from the British Library

ISBN 978 1 84866 518 7
ebook ISBN 978 1 84866 519 4

1 3 5 7 9 10 8 6 4 2

Printed and bound in Great Britain by Clays Ltd, St Ives plc.

For Jo
J.G.

For Wen
A.S.

For Iris and JJ
S.H.

contents

1
TV Troubles

'It's my turn!' said Coco.

'No, it's not. It's my turn!' said Fuzzy.

'But you've been on it for ages!'

'That's because YOU were on it for ages!'

Fuzzy and Coco were guinea pigs. They lived in the kitchen at number 7,

Middleton Crescent, Strawberry Park.
And they were arguing over the laptop.

'I have to see the latest episode of
The Ice Factor,' said Coco.

'No, you don't. You've seen it loads
of times already,' said Fuzzy.

'No, I haven't. I've only seen it eight
times and I like to see each episode ten
times.'

'Well, I've only seen this episode of
Winter Warmers ONCE and I need to
see it again because I want to make
Volcano Veg for dinner.'

'Well, I don't want Volcano Veg for
dinner,' said Coco.

'Well, you don't have to have any,' said Fuzzy.

'Well, good. So can I watch *The Ice Factor* now?'

'No.'

Luckily at that moment the catflap opened and Terry, their guinea-pig friend from next door, popped through it. He was covered in a light sprinkling of snow. Fuzzy and Coco went to greet him.

'Hi, Terry, are you OK?' said Fuzzy. 'You look cold.'

'I'm fine, thanks, Fuz,' Terry said, pulling off his woolly hat and giving it a quick shake, before putting it back on again. Terry always wore his hat, even indoors.

'It must be freezing out there in the hutch,' Coco said. 'How's your mum? And all your brothers and sisters?' Terry had thirteen little brothers and sisters and a wonderful mum called Banoffee, who was one of Coco's best friends.

'We're all fine,' answered Terry.

'Our owners have moved us into a new hutch in the house to keep warm.'

Both Fuzzy and Coco sighed with relief.

'Oh good!' said Coco. 'We've been so worried about you. It said on the news that this is the coldest winter since the last coldest winter.'

'No, it didn't,' said Fuzzy.

'Yes, it did,' Coco said. 'You weren't watching.'

'That's because *you* were watching, even though it was *my* turn.'

'No, it wasn't.'

'Yes, it was.'

'No, it wasn't.'

'Excuse me,' said Terry, who was very sensible, even though he was younger than Coco and Fuzzy, 'but why doesn't one of you watch on the TV in the lounge? Then you wouldn't argue about it.' Terry also liked TV and computers, so he knew what he was talking about.

'That's a good idea,' said Coco, 'but this is the only room Ben and Henrietta heat for us while they're at work. It's freezing in the lounge.'

Ben and Henrietta were Fuzzy and Coco's owners. Ben worked at the animal rescue centre. Henrietta was a vet.

'So why doesn't one of you watch your TV programme on the phone?' Terry said. 'Ben and Hen usually leave one lying around, don't they?' Ben and Henrietta were very forgetful.

'That's a great idea!' said Coco, dashing over to the phone and turning it on. 'Have you seen *The Ice Factor*, Terry? It's the most brilliant programme. They have an ice skater and a celebrity, and they have to dance together in a competition.'

'And when they fall over they cry, and when they win they cry, and when they lose they cry . . .' said Fuzzy.

'At least it's better than your silly *Winter Warmers* programme,' Coco shot back. 'That's boring. All they do on that is cook.'

'No, they don't. They have a cook and a celebrity and they have to cook together in a competition.'

'Sounds a bit like *The Ice Factor*,' said Terry.

Coco peered at the phone screen. She needed glasses, but she refused to wear them.

'I can't watch on this. The screen is too small. It makes the dancers look like ants.'

'Maybe *you* could watch on the phone, Fuzzy,' suggested Terry.

'That won't work,' said Fuzzy. 'I won't be able to see what the contestants are cooking.'

'You could zoom in,' suggested Terry.

'No, I can't,' said Fuzzy.

'Yes, you can,' said Terry.

'No, I can't,' said Fuzzy.

Now Fuzzy and Terry were arguing!

'Stop arguing with Terry!' said Coco.

'OK,' said Fuzzy to Coco. 'I'll argue with you instead.'

Just then the catflap opened once more. This time a big round snowball came hurtling through it and landed on the kitchen floor. The three guinea pigs looked at it in surprise.

'Where did that come from?' said Fuzzy.

'Perhaps one of the kids next door threw it in,' said Terry.

Just then the snowball started to wriggle.

'It's alive!' shrieked Coco.

The snowball muttered and groaned.

'*Madre mía*,' it said.

'It can speak Spanish!' said Fuzzy.

The snowball was wriggling and groaning and muttering in Spanish.

Flakes of snow flicked in all directions.
They fell on the kitchen floor and
started to melt. Then dollops of snow
dropped to the ground. Coco, Fuzzy
and Terry could see that underneath
the snow was a guinea pig with black
fur speckled with silver.

'It's Eduardo!' Coco exclaimed.

Eduardo was another one of Fuzzy and Coco's friends. He was a type of guinea pig called an Agouti. He came from Peru, but now he lived in a burrow in the copse at the bottom of Coco and Fuzzy's garden.

Eduardo stamped his paws so that the last bits of snow fell from his legs. He shook his satchel to dry it off. There were now quite large pools of water on the kitchen floor.

'You're making a terrible mess, Eduardo. Could you go back outside and do that?' asked Coco.

Coco wasn't always very nice to

Eduardo. This was because secretly she really liked him so she tried too hard to impress him and it came out all wrong.

Eduardo looked at her in astonishment. 'Outside, *señorita*? OUTSIDE?' he cried. 'Have you been outside recently?'

'Well, no, to be honest,' Coco admitted. 'It's far too cold and snowy. I'd rather be in here in the warm.'

'*Exactamente, señorita*! It is very cold and very snowy outside. That is why I am come inside to see you!'

'Have you got enough to eat?' Fuzzy asked.

'*Nada*,' said Eduardo sadly. '*No hay nada para comer.*'

'Has the cold got to your brain?' asked Coco. 'You seem to have forgotten how to speak English.'

'I have not forgotten nothing,' Eduardo chuttered, sounding cross. 'But I have no energy to speak English because I am hungry. *No hay nada para comer* means there is nothing to eat.'

'That's odd.' Fuzzy frowned. 'Ben's been making special oat cookies and Henrietta's been putting them out in the copse for the wild animals every morning before work.'

'I find no food, *amigo*. And all my
friends they find no food. The robin
he find no food, the mouse she find no
food. We all are hungry.'

'Do you know what I'm thinking?'
said Coco.

'No, I do not. I cannot read your mind,' said Eduardo.

'I think someone is taking your food.'

'Who?' Eduardo demanded. 'Who, who, who do this?'

'Someone large and red and—'

'Father Christmas!' guessed Terry.

'No!' said Coco. 'He doesn't take things, he gives them. He gave me a lovely pink bow for Christmas.'

'Coco means the fox,' Fuzzy said, 'not Father Christmas, don't you, Coco?'

'Renard the fox!' said Terry. 'You're

right. It's just the sort of sneaky thing he'd do. I'll bet it's him.'

'But what are we going to do about it?' Coco said. 'I mean, we can't just march out there and tell him to stop or he'll eat us instead.'

At the thought of Renard they all fell silent. They turned and looked out of the French windows into the garden. Snow was falling softly. Icicles hung from the kitchen roof. It was getting dark. None of them wanted to go out into the cold to look for a large, mean creature who wanted to eat *them*.

'Let's have a think about it while

I fix Eduardo something to eat,' Fuzzy suggested.

'*Gracias, amigo.*' Eduardo bowed.

'I'll help,' Terry offered.

The two guinea pigs pattered off towards the fridge.

'That's a good idea,' Coco called after them. 'You two go and do that and I'll catch up on my TV programme.' She turned back to the laptop.

Fuzzy sighed. Coco could be a bit selfish sometimes. But she was too selfish to *realize* that she was being selfish.

Coco was scrolling through the shows.

Eduardo sat down beside her. His eye fell on one of the titles. 'Hah!' he cried. '*The Butch Grizzly Show*! My favourite! I used to watch it in Peru.'

And before Coco could stop him, he clicked *play*.

2
Volcano Veg

'Welcome to Norway,' a voice said. The film showed a pair of big lace-up boots tramping through deep snow.

Coco yawned. 'Is he going to do any skating?' she asked. 'I need to watch *The Ice Factor*, you know.'

Eduardo was glued to the screen.

'Shhhh!'

'Here I am in search of food,' the voice said. 'It's been hours since my last meal. And that was only puffin droppings.'

Coco pulled a face.

'I know how you feel, *hombre*!' Eduardo muttered. 'It's been hours since my last meal too.'

'Why doesn't he just go to the shop,' Coco asked, 'if he's hungry?'

Eduardo blinked. 'Shop? What shop? There are no shops in the Arctic. In the Arctic you must hunt and forage for food in order to survive.' He wriggled his bushy eyebrows at her. 'Man, you pet guinea pigs crack me up sometimes! Shops?! Pah!'

'All right,' Coco said, 'keep your eyebrows on.' She yawned again. 'I don't think I'd like the Arctic if there aren't any shops.'

'Shhhh!' Eduardo glared at her. 'Listen!'

'But I must be careful,' the voice went on. 'If the polar bear sees me, it will attack.' The camera jolted. A man appeared on the screen and squatted down in front of the camera. Coco gave a little shudder. He had long hair and a wild beard. He wore a fur hat with earflaps, a thick padded coat and fingerless gloves. He didn't look anything like the celebrities on *The Ice Factor*.

'Where's his sparkly costume?' she complained.

'He doesn't have a sparkly costume,' Eduardo snapped. 'He would freeze to death.'

'What about his ice skates?' Coco said.

'Butch Grizzly has no use for ice skates!' Eduardo rounded on her. 'He is an adventurer, like me.' He settled back down.

'There's no need to shout!' Coco said. Then after a few seconds she added, 'I should think ice skates would be very useful if you were trying to get away from a polar bear. I mean you could skate really fast across the ice so that the polar bear couldn't catch you.'

'Shhhhh!' Eduardo put his paws up to block his ears. Then he realized that he couldn't hear Butch Grizzly, so he put them down again.

Butch Grizzly was studying the ground. 'Flipper prints!' he hissed. He stuck his finger in a pile of something brown and licked it. 'Mmmm,' he said. 'Fresh walrus dung! Delicious on mouldy toast.' He removed a bit of frozen bread from his pocket and waved it at the camera. It had blue spots all over it.

'Eeuwwww!' Coco let out a shriek of horror. 'He's not actually going to eat mouldy bread and walrus dung, is he?'

'He is so cool!' Eduardo sighed.

Just then Fuzzy and Terry arrived with Eduardo's food. They pushed a bowl of chopped vegetables in front of him. 'Here you go, Eduardo,' Fuzzy said. 'It's one of the recipes from *Winter Warmers*, the cooking show. It's called Volcano Veg.' He scratched his crest. 'I hope I remembered the recipe right.'

Eduardo grunted his thanks. He reached out a paw and grabbed some food, stuffed it in his mouth and began to chew.

'Do you like it?' Fuzzy asked.

Eduardo's nose had gone from pink to bright red. His eyes watered. 'Hot, hot, hot!' he panted.

'What's the matter?' Coco said, alarmed. 'Is he on fire?'

'Aarrrgggghhhh!' Eduardo clutched
at his throat. 'It's burning . . .'

'Quick!' Coco said. 'Do something
before he goes up in smoke!'

Terry struggled up with a beaker
of water. 'Get him away from the

computer!' he shouted. 'We mustn't get the laptop wet or it won't work any more.'

Fuzzy threw himself on top of Eduardo and kicked out with his legs. The two guinea pigs rolled along the kitchen tiles.

'Here it comes!'

Fuzzy leaped out of the way.

Terry threw the water over Eduardo. SPLOSH!

Eduardo struggled to his feet. His black fur was bedraggled. 'It is not my body that's on fire!' he gurgled. 'It is my mouth!' He dunked his head in the beaker and drank what was left of the water.

'His mouth?' Coco echoed. 'How come?'

'Oh dear!' Fuzzy said, looking at the plate of chopped vegetables. 'I think I might have put a bit too much chilli in the Volcano Veg.'

'I am not chilly!' Eduardo's wet nose emerged from the beaker. 'I tell you I am hot!'

'No, Eduardo, a chilli is a very

spicy pepper,' Coco explained. 'That's why your mouth feels like it's on fire. Fuzzy put too much in the Volcano Veg because he got the recipe wrong.'

' I told you I wanted to watch *Winter Warmers* again and you wouldn't let me!' Fuzzy fumed at Coco. 'It was your fault!'

'No, it wasn't!'

'Yes, it was!'

'No, it wasn't!'

'Here we go again!' Terry sighed.

'*Amigos*,' Eduardo said sadly, 'I do not think I am welcome here. First Coco, she insults my hero, Butch

Grizzly. Then my good friend Fuzzy sets fire to my mouth with something he says is chilly that is not cold at all but very hot. I think perhaps you are making fun of me.'

'But we're not!' Fuzzy said. 'I'm really sorry, Eduardo!'

'So am I,' Coco said in a small voice. And she was too. Even silly Coco could see that Eduardo was upset. 'Fuzzy will make you something else to eat, won't you, Fuzzy?'

'Don't bother, *amigo*.' Eduardo shook his head. 'I must go back to my friends in the copse. I must teach them

to forage for food like Butch Grizzly.'
He sighed. '*Adios, amigos*. See you in
the spring.' He disappeared out of the
catflap without another word.

'Now look what you've done!'
Coco said to Fuzzy.

'What do you mean, what I've
done?! It's what you've done!' Fuzzy
said.

'Stop it!' Terry said crossly. 'We need
to do something to help the animals in
the copse.'

'Terry's right, Coco,' Fuzzy said.
'Then Eduardo will forgive us.'

'All right,' Coco agreed. 'But what

can we do if the fox is taking the food
that Ben and Henrietta are leaving
out? We don't have enough to spare for
everyone.'

'Let's do what we always do when
we're in trouble,' Terry said. 'Let's go
on Micespace.' Micespace was the
way the guinea pigs kept in touch
with all their animal friends online.

'We'll ask for help. We can ask everyone to donate some food. They can bring it to our old hutch in the morning. It's big enough for everyone to fit in.'

'That's a brilliant idea, Terry!' Fuzzy said.

'If everyone gives a little bit, none of our owners will notice the food is missing,' Coco exclaimed.

Terry nodded. 'That's what I figure. They'll just think we're extra hungry because of the cold.'

'I can make my Volcano Veg, but this time with the right amount of chilli!' Fuzzy said.

'Yeah, well, we'll see about that,' Terry said. 'Now let's get on the computer and spread the word.'

3
Coco's Big Idea

Early next morning, when Fuzzy and Coco were still fast asleep, there was a little tap on the door of their hutch. Fuzzy woke first.

'Who's there?' he said, his eyes still closed.

'It's Pepper,' said the small voice.

Pepper was the second youngest of Banoffee's children.

'Oh, hello, Pepper!' said Fuzzy, opening his eyes and getting up all in one go. 'What brings you visiting so early in the morning?'

'I've brought you a lettuce leaf,' said Pepper.

The lettuce leaf was almost bigger than Pepper, so Fuzzy could only just see her little paws peeking out from behind it.

'That is kind of you. Thank you,' said Fuzzy.

'It's not actually for you. It's for

the poor, hungry wild animals in the copse,' said Pepper.

'I know,' said Fuzzy. 'And I'll give it to them. Thank you.'

'We read on Micespace that you're collecting food. I know it's supposed to go to our old hutch in the garden but I couldn't wait any longer so Mum said I could bring it to you here.'

'That's fine. And it's very kind of you. I'll take it down to the hutch later and give it to the wild animals there. Thank you. Bye-bye.'

'Bye,' said Pepper. She laid the lettuce leaf on the kitchen floor and made her way back out of the cat flap. Fuzzy fell back on the soft hay and went back to sleep.

A few seconds later there was another little knock on the hutch door. This time it was Coco who woke up. The visitor was Blossom, Banoffee's youngest daughter.

'I've brought some seeds for the wild animals in the copse,' she said.

'That *is* kind of you,' said Coco in a nice voice, even though she didn't feel like being nice because she had been woken up much earlier than usual.

Once Blossom had gone, Coco went back to sleep too, but not for long. There was another knock on the hutch door. It was another one of Banoffee's children. After that, there was another and then another, all bringing food for the wild animals in the copse. Eventually, after visits from all of Banoffee's children (apart from Terry who was busy fixing up the Wi-Fi in the old hutch), Fuzzy and Coco gave up trying to sleep and got up. While they were eating their breakfast more donations arrived from local pets.

'Give us a hand with this food, will
you, Coco?' Fuzzy said. 'I've got to get
it all down to Banoffee's hutch so we
can give it to the wild animals.'

Coco gave a huge yawn. 'I'm much

too tired to help, Fuzzy,' she said. 'I need to catch up on all the beauty sleep I've missed by being woken so early.'

So Fuzzy took all the donated food down to the hutch (he had to make the journey a few times because there was so much of it) while Coco tried to go back to sleep. But she was wide awake now, so while Fuzzy was out of the house she sneaked off to watch *The Ice Factor* on the laptop.

It was then that she had her brilliant idea. She switched from *The Ice Factor* to Micespace and carefully typed a message:

The *Ice Factor* comes to Strawberry Park!

Come on down to the Ice-Skating Competition

When: later today. RSVP*
Where: the frozen stream in the copse
Dress: sparkly

*RSVP is French for let me know if you can make it.

Coco clicked on the box marked *Send* and scuttled off to look for her tiara. When she came back to check the computer she was excited to see that lots of animals had already accepted her invitation. The computer gave another ping. *New message* flashed up on the screen. And underneath it said:

Rufus and Renarta are pleased to accept your invitation.

Coco didn't know Rufus and Renarta. They must be friends of Fuzzy's, she thought. But she knew she should be sensible and ask some questions just in case. So she typed:

Are you guinea pigs?

No. We are hairs.

Hairs?

No. Sorry. Hares.

Ha ha. That's funny. I didn't think hairs could skate! Coco wrote.

We are last year's Strawberry Park ice-skating champions and we can teach you how to skate.

Great! I'll see you on the frozen stream later. Don't forget your sparkly costume.

Coco rushed outside and down to Banoffee's old hutch to tell Fuzzy and Terry about the ice-skating competition. Luckily it had stopped snowing, but it was still very cold. By the time she got to the hutch her teeth were chattering.

'Fuzzy, I've had the m-m-most br-br-brilliant idea!'

'Hang on a minute, Coco, I'm just dishing up,' said Fuzzy.

Coco looked around her. The hutch was divided into two parts. In the bedroom part Terry was organizing the different foods into neat piles: lettuce, seeds, carrots and so on. Next to the raw food was a pot of Fuzzy's Volcano Veg, but with the right amount of chilli in it this time. In the living space stood an orderly queue of wild animals. There was a mouse, then a robin, then Olaf, the guinea pig who liked to pretend he was a Viking, then lots of other animals from the copse. Fuzzy stood at the

doorway between the two parts of the
hutch, dishing out the food.

'What would you like to eat?' Fuzzy
asked the mouse.

'Have you got any cheese?'

'Sorry, I'm afraid not.'

'How about lettuce?'

'Yes, we have,' said Fuzzy. 'Lettuce,
please, Terry.'

'Lettuce coming up,' said Terry, as he
passed the lettuce to
Fuzzy, who passed
it to the mouse.

'Thanks a
million,' said the mouse.

'Enjoy your meal,' said Fuzzy. 'Who's next?'

'It's me,' said Olaf the Viking. 'Have you got any Viking meat stew?'

'No, because this is a vegetarian soup kitchen,' said Fuzzy.

'OK, then I'll have some vegetarian soup.'

'No, Olaf,' said Fuzzy, 'a soup kitchen is a place that feeds hungry animals. We don't actually have any soup. But my Volcano Veg is good.'

'I'll try that then,' said Olaf, taking off his helmet and holding it out to Fuzzy so he could ladle his food into it.

'A Viking is always prepared,' he said.

After a while Banoffee took over
handing out the food.

'So what's your brilliant idea?'
Fuzzy asked Coco.

'*The Ice Factor* comes to the copse!' said Coco proudly.

'Does it?' asked Fuzzy. 'So we'll be invaded by TV cameras and sparkly costumes?'

'Not the real *Ice Factor*!' said Coco. 'I thought we could have our own *Ice Factor* competition in the copse and I could wear my tiara *and* my silver bow and perhaps have a bit of tinsel as a scarf—'

'So what's the point of *The Ice Factor* in the copse,' said Fuzzy, 'apart from giving you the chance to show off?'

'It's not for me to show off!' Coco

protested (even though showing off *had* been her first idea). 'It's for all the wild animals to keep warm. I read on the Internet that you don't just need food to survive the cold, you need to keep moving. Otherwise you get hippo-thermometer.'

'*Hypo*thermia,' said Terry, who used an online speaking dictionary so he knew how words sounded as well as how to spell them.

'Whatever,' said Coco. 'It means you get so cold you can't talk.' She shuddered at the thought of such a dreadful fate. 'I've posted an invitation on Micespace to all our animal friends, telling them to come down to the frozen stream for our very own *Ice Factor* competition.'

'That's amazing, Coco. I remember when you hated computers,' said Fuzzy. 'And now you're posting invitations on Micespace!'

'I've had lots of replies already, including one from a pair of hares called Rufus and Renarta who were last year's Strawberry Park ice-skating champions.'

'Rufus and Renarta? I don't remember them,' said Fuzzy.

'Come on, Fuzzy – you've got so many friends on Micespace, you can't remember them all,' said Coco. 'I checked anyway. They seem really nice. They're going to teach me how to skate!'

4
The Soup Kitchen

For the rest of the morning Fuzzy and his helpers were rushed off their paws as word spread around the copse about the soup kitchen. Luckily donations of food kept arriving as the kindly pets of Strawberry Park rallied round to help.

'Give us a paw, Coco!' Fuzzy puffed.

It was hard work making enough Volcano Veg to feed everyone.

'Yes, don't just sit there mooning about *The Ice Factor*!' Banoffee was helping Fuzzy chop more veg. 'Here you go!' She threw some carrots into the bowl.

'Thanks, Mum!' Blossom and Pepper were taking it in turns to do the stirring.

'I'm not mooning!' Coco said. 'I'm just thinking about my dance routine. And anyway, don't be bossy!' Normally it was Coco who bossed Banoffee about, not the other way around.

'Next batch coming up!' Fuzzy shouted.

'Here, grab this, Co.' Terry thrust a bowl into Coco's paws. 'You can help serve.'

Coco sighed. The soup kitchen was

all well and good, but it wasn't much *fun*!
Not as much fun as watching *The Ice
Factor* anyway. Still, once everyone had
had something to eat, she was pretty sure
that they'd want to do some ice dancing,
and then Rufus and Renarta would
teach her how to do it, and when they
all saw how brilliant she was, everyone
would clap ...

ENCORE
ENCORE!
BRAVO!

'Do you have any cream to go with that?' A smooth voice interrupted her daydream. A very large squirrel had reached the front of the food queue. Except it wasn't standing on its back legs like squirrels normally do. Instead it sat very calmly licking one of its paws. And it was wearing a grey playsuit, with a hood and a long bushy squirrel tail.

'Cream?' Coco repeated. She looked at the squirrel suspiciously. There was something familiar about its big green eyes and long white whiskers. She was sure she'd seen it somewhere before. For a moment she thought it might be

Renard. But although it was big for a squirrel, it wasn't big enough for a fox.

'Or fish?' the squirrel purred hopefully.

Coco frowned. Squirrels didn't eat cream. Or fish, for that matter. And they didn't purr. She looked at the animal more closely. Then she realized. It was Alan the cat from next door on the other side! He had disguised himself as a squirrel so he could get some grub! 'What are you doing here, Alan?' she demanded. 'The soup kitchen is for wild animals only!'

'I am wild,' Alan insisted. 'I'm wild about food.'

'Nice try, Alan,' Fuzzy said, coming over, 'but we know it's you. Where did you get the squirrel disguise?'

'It's a onesie,' Alan explained proudly. 'My owners gave it to me for my birthday. They're all the rage at Pets2Go.' Pets2Go was the local pet shop. Ben and Henrietta often went there to buy things for Coco and Fuzzy.

'Do you think they've got a sparkly pink one that I could wear for skating?' Coco asked.

Just then there was a commotion at the back of the food queue. 'Come on, everyone!' a voice shouted. 'Let's have some fun!'

Fun! Coco's ears pricked up. That was more like it.

'Is that Eduardo?' Fuzzy said. The voice had a Spanish accent.

The sound of a guitar filled the hutch.

'No!' Coco cried joyfully. 'It's not Eduardo. It's Bernardo!'

Bernardo was Eduardo's cousin from Peru. Coco and Fuzzy hadn't seen him for ages.

'*Hola, señorita!*' Bernardo made his way through the crush. He looked exactly like Eduardo except that his silver-speckled fur was chocolate brown (instead of black) and he had a guitar slung over his shoulder. 'May I say you're looking lovelier than ever?' He kissed her paw.

'You may!' Coco replied. Bernardo had lovely manners.

'Bernardo!' Fuzzy gave him a hug. 'What are you doing here?'

'I'm on tour,' Bernardo explained. 'I've written some new songs and I'm travelling from country to country singing them to all the guinea pigs I meet.'

'Cool, dude!' said Terry, who had only seen Bernardo on the webcam. 'I'll help you do a video if you like. We can post it on the Internet.'

'You're on, my friend!' Bernardo cried. 'Now you tell me – what is happening in here? Did Fuzzy start a restaurant? I know he likes to cook.'

'Not quite!' Quickly Fuzzy explained about watching *Winter Warmers* and about the animals in the copse going hungry and how they thought the fox had been stealing the food that Ben and Henrietta put out. 'So we set up a soup kitchen,' he said proudly, 'and got everyone to donate something.'

Bernardo brushed a tear away from his eye. '*Amigo*, that is the most beautiful thing I have ever heard in my life, apart from my songs.'

'And I'm organizing an ice-dancing competition!' Coco told him, not to be outdone. And quickly she explained about watching *The Ice Factor* and about going on Micespace to invite all the animals to the competition and about Rufus and Renarta, the hare ice-skating champions, and how they were going to teach her how to skate.

Bernardo let out a whoop of joy. '*The Ice Factor!* I love that show! We get it on the laptop in Peru.'

Fuzzy frowned. 'It's not as good as *Winter Warmers*.'

'Yes, it is!' Coco interrupted. A fantastic idea suddenly occurred to her. 'Bernardo, would you be my partner in the skating competition? You could be the celebrity if you like,' she added generously, 'seeing as you're a famous pop star.'

'I would be honoured, *señorita*,' Bernardo said. 'Now, to cheer everyone up I will sing you one of my wonderful songs.' He strummed his guitar loudly. 'Let's party, *amigos*! Let's rock this joint!'

All the animals cheered and clapped as Bernardo launched into a jaunty song.

'He's really good!' Coco laughed in delight.

Fuzzy's whiskers twitched in time to the music.

Terry was doing a little dance with his mum. Their bottoms waggled. All his brothers and sisters joined in. So did the other animals.

'*I am Bernardo and I love to rock and roll,*
Now I'm feeling hungry
so please give me a bowl!
Fuzzy's my mate and
he knows how to cook,
And Señorita Coco is the one with the looks!'

'Come on, everyone! After me!'
Bernardo started the tune again. This time everyone joined in, including Alan.

'Here in the soup kitchen
we love to rock and roll,
We live in the copse
and we go for a stroll,
Out in the woods
we sing and we hum,
And when we get home
we start banging a drum!'

Suddenly the door to the hutch
opened again and Eduardo marched in.
He looked very cross. Everyone stopped
singing.

'What's going on?' he demanded.

'Bernardo's come all the way

from Peru!' Coco gushed. 'He's going to be my partner in *The Ice Factor* competition.'

'He's on a music tour!' Fuzzy told him. 'He's written a song about my cooking.'

'We're gonna shoot a video!' Terry explained. 'And post it on the Internet.'

'I see,' Eduardo said slowly. He paced up and down shaking his head. Suddenly he stopped. 'And you all think this is more important than survival?'

'Of course not, Eduardo,' Fuzzy said.

'We were just having a bit of fun,' Coco added.

'Fun? FUN!' Eduardo shouted.
'You think it is fun for me to be out there in the cold wilderness foraging for food? You think it is fun to eat your own droppings and build an igloo out of packed ice using only your toenails and a bunch of skeleton keys?'

'But you don't have to, mate!' Terry pointed out. 'You could be in the hutch keeping warm like the rest of us.'

'No.' Eduardo shook his head again. This time it was he who launched into song.

'I am Eduardo, I'm brave and I'm bold,
I don't feel no fear and I don't feel no cold,
Butch Grizzly is my hero and I'll never shirk
Survival in the wilderness is my kind of work.'

'It's good,' Coco said, 'but it's not as good as Bernardo's.'

Eduardo looked even more furious than ever. 'You have not been listening, *señorita*. It is a protest song. My place is out there in the wilderness, like my hero Butch Grizzly. The soup kitchen will not last forever. I must forage and build. I must defeat Renard so that he no longer steals the food that is meant for us. I must find other animals who do not know about the soup kitchen. Who is with me? Who? Who? Who?'

Everyone looked at the floor.

Suddenly a little voice spoke up. 'I'll come!' It was Blossom.

'So will I!' It was Pepper.

'Very well,' Eduardo agreed. 'You may join me on this dangerous mission. I commend your bravery. Unlike some others I could mention.' He shot a filthy look at Coco, Fuzzy and Bernardo.

'I'll make you a packed lunch,' Fuzzy said.

He did that while Banoffee fussed about with coats and hats and mittens. 'Don't catch cold,' she warned Blossom and Pepper.

'We won't!'

'And take a tissue in case you get a runny nose!'

'We will!'

Eduardo nodded approvingly at his two helpers. He grabbed his lunch. 'Come, my friends,' he said. 'We will take the truck.'

5
The Snow Truck

The truck was a toy that someone had dumped in the copse.

'The truck looks different,' said Pepper.

'That's because I have turned it into a snow plough, like we have in the mountains of Peru.'

'It looks like you've tied a ruler on the front,' said Pepper.

'I have,' said Eduardo. 'I found it on the ground. The ruler will scrape the snow and make a path for the truck.'

'Can we get in?' asked Blossom.

'Of course,' said Eduardo, and helped them up into the cab.

The young guinea pigs liked sitting in the truck. Eduardo sat behind the wheel and started up the engine. Luckily there was still some power left in the batteries. The truck moved off through the snow. It worked just like a snow plough because the ruler tied to the front cleared the snow in its path.

It was very quiet in the copse. Snow lay thick on the trees and plants.

'Shall I call out to all the hungry animals?' asked Pepper.

'Please, *amiga*,' said Eduardo.

'Ha-llo! Ha-llo-ho!' called Pepper.

No one called back.

Blossom joined in.

'HA-LLO! HA-LLO-HO!' called the young guinea pigs.

Silence.

'Perhaps everyone who is hungry has gone to the soup kitchen already,' suggested Blossom.

'Perhaps,' agreed Eduardo.

'*HOLA! HOLA-HOLA-HOLA-HOLLLAAAAAAA!*' he shouted at the top of his voice.

GGGGRRRRRAAAA!

Suddenly they all heard a loud groan.

GGGRRRRRAAAA!

The groan was coming from a pile of leaves.

'Shall we call again?' Pepper asked Eduardo.

'There's no need. I'm awake now,' said a grumpy voice.

The leaves began to move and a little black nose appeared, followed by two little black eyes and some brown spikes.

'It's a hedgehog!' said Pepper.

'Oh no, we've woken it up,' said
Blossom.

'So what's the problem, *amigas*?'

Eduardo said to the little guinea pigs.
And then, to the hedgehog: 'Come,
friend, we take you somewhere warm,
where you can eat!'

'I am already somewhere warm,'
said the hedgehog. 'And I don't want to
eat. I want to sleep.'

'Sleep? But it is dinner-time,' said
Eduardo.

'Hedgehogs sleep all winter,'
Blossom whispered to Eduardo. 'It's
called hibernation.'

'Ah, now I understand,' said
Eduardo. 'We don't have these hog-
hedges in Peru.'

He reversed the truck away from the pile of leaves.

'Goodnight, *amigo*, see you in the spring!' Eduardo called.

'Goodnight!' called Blossom and Pepper.

The truck set off through the copse again. The three guinea pigs looked carefully into the undergrowth to see if there were any hungry animals who wanted food, unlike the hedgehog who only wanted sleep. Before they had gone very far the ruler on the front of the truck hit something hard. Eduardo stopped the truck and jumped down from the cab. He walked around to the front, then bent down to feel the ground under the snow.

'Ah, tree roots! We must check in the burrows underneath. Maybe there are hungry rabbits too weak to call out. Come!'

He beckoned to Blossom and Pepper. The tree roots led to a big old horse chestnut. There was a split in the trunk wide enough for the guinea pigs to climb through. Eduardo led the way. Blossom and Pepper followed, although they were both a little scared.

'Are you sure this is safe?' whispered Blossom.

'Of course it's safe,' said Eduardo. 'You're with me.'

Inside the tree trunk it was very dark but the earth was dry. The two baby guinea pigs sniffed.

They all noticed the stink but it was Pepper who spoke up. 'It smells disgusting in here,' she said.

'Yes, it does,' said Eduardo, 'but we must help all animals, even the stinky ones.'

The smell was coming from a hole beneath them. Eduardo led the way

down. The little guinea pigs followed.
The stink got worse.

'Pooh!' said Pepper.

'Put your scarf over your nose. That
will help,' said Blossom.

Pepper did as she was told.

When they reached the bottom of
the hole, the guinea pigs saw that they
were in a large burrow.

Here the stink was particularly bad. Even Eduardo held his nose with his paw while he looked around.

'I wonder who lives here,' said Blossom.

There were animal tracks on the ground. Some chewed bones lay in a bowl next to a bed of feathers. In a corner was a tablet computer. Eduardo crept over to it. He pressed a key with his paw and the screen sprang to life. The guinea pigs crowded around.

~● ▷ **MICESPACE**

The *Ice Factor* comes to Strawberry Park!

'Whoever it is has seen Coco's invitation,' said Pepper. 'They must be coming to the ice-skating competition.'

'What ice-skating competition?' Eduardo asked.

The two little guinea pigs told him.

Eduardo's face was sombre. 'Come, *amigas*, we have no time to lose.'

'But what's the matter?' asked Blossom.

'I'll tell you on the way.'

The three guinea pigs raced out of the burrow and jumped back in the truck.

6
Things get Harey!

'You can't tell my kids they must vote for you! You might not be any good!' said Banoffee.

'Of course I'll be good! I'll be better than you anyway!' said Coco.

Back at the soup kitchen a row had broken out between Banoffee and Coco over *The Ice Factor* competition. Coco desperately wanted to win and she had been trying to persuade Banoffee's children to vote for her.

'No, you won't!' Banoffee said. 'I've watched it on the telly just as much as you have. I know all the moves.'

'I don't believe you,' said Coco. 'Prove it!'

'All right, I will.' Banoffee took a running jump and leaped into the air. She landed on top of Fuzzy.

'Oomph!' Fuzzy groaned.

'See!' Coco gloated. 'I knew you weren't very good.'

'That's because there's no ice, dummy!' Banoffee picked herself up.

'Don't call me dummy,' Coco shouted, 'or I'll call you fatty!'

The two guinea pigs glared at one another.

'Ladies, ladies!' Bernardo said. 'This

isn't a wrestling match in a Peruvian mudslide. It's a dance competition, remember?' He licked his paws and smoothed the fur on his cheeks. 'We must be cool. We must be elegant. Now come. Let's go to the stream for a practice.'

'But I don't have a partner,' Banoffee said sadly.

'Ha ha, serves you right!' Coco crowed.

'I'll be your partner,' Fuzzy offered kindly.

'That's brave of you!' Coco sniggered. 'I wouldn't like to be in your paws when fatty lands on you. It would be like being run over by a bus.'

'Stop it, Coco!' Fuzzy said sharply. 'Guinea pigs come in all shapes and sizes. Don't be mean about Banoffee. She's one of your best friends.'

Coco realized that everyone was looking at her. And not at all in the admiring way she had hoped. She felt very small and silly. She burst into tears. 'I'm sorry, Banoffee,' she said, tears streaming down her face.

'That's all right!' Banoffee sprang forward at once and gave her a hug. 'I'm sorry too. What we need is some fresh air. I've been cooped up for so long this winter I think I've gone a bit mad!'

'Me too!' Coco sniffed.

'But then again, it's so cold,' Banoffee started to worry, 'I don't think we should go out without extra clothes on.'

'Honestly, Mum, you do make a fuss!' Terry said. 'But if you're that worried about it, we could always raid the dressing-up box.'

'The dressing-up box?!' Coco echoed.

'Yeah, it's full of old doll's clothes,' Terry explained. 'The kids from the house used to try and dress us up in them sometimes.' He chuckled. 'They never twigged that we could do it on our own when they weren't looking!'

'I love dressing up,' Coco said dreamily.

'So do we!' chorused Banoffee's children.

'The box is over there,' Banoffee said, pointing to the corner of the hutch.

'Give me a hand, Alan,' Terry said. 'You're the biggest.'

'I'm also the laziest,' Alan reminded him, lying down for a nap. 'And I'm already dressed up as a squirrel.'

'I'll help,' Fuzzy offered.

'By the might of Mordor, so will I!'
Olaf the Viking guinea pig agreed.

The three guinea pigs pulled and
tugged at the old box. After a little
while they had pulled it into the
centre of the hutch. Fuzzy lifted the lid.
Everyone crowded around.

'Oh, Banoffee, they're wonderful!'
Coco gasped.

Inside the box was an assortment
of clothes. There were even shoes and a
pair of white skating boots!

As soon as she saw the skating
boots Coco knew that she wanted them

more than anything else in the world,
but because she'd just been told off, she
didn't dare ask for them.

Fuzzy chose a warm scarf. Terry
found some mittens. Bernardo wrapped
himself in a silver cloak. Banoffee
decided on a pink woolly cardigan

with big shiny buttons and a pair of
elasticated blue knickers. Then all
Banoffee's other children selected
something. Coco began to wonder if
there would be anything left for her to
wear at all, never mind if she'd get the
skating boots.

'Don't worry!' Banoffee whispered. 'There's still something special in there for you!'

Coco looked into the box. In among the dull woolly clothes there was a tiny bit of shiny blue poking out. She pulled at it and drew out a spangly ice-blue leotard. It was the perfect costume for *The Ice Factor*!

'Put it on then!'

Coco wriggled into it. It was quite hard getting her legs into the right holes. The first time she ended up with the bottom bit over her head, and her bottom poking out where her head should be, but after a few tries and a little bit of help from Banoffee, she got it on the right way round.

'You look very nice,' Banoffee said.

'So do you!' Coco lied. The knickers and pink cardy looked completely daft, but she didn't want to upset Banoffee again.

'Thanks, Coco. 'Here –' she held out the skating boots 'I want you to wear these.'

Coco almost burst into tears for a second time. She had such good friends after all! She promised herself she would never be silly and selfish again.

'Follow me, everyone!' She couldn't wait to impress Rufus and Renarta with her costume!

The guinea pigs scampered out of the hutch and off towards the stream.

'It's not as easy as it looks!' Banoffee panted.

'You can say that again!' Coco puffed. To her surprise, the skates didn't seem to be helping.

'I would do, but I'm too out of breath!' Banoffee gasped.

The two guinea pigs slipped and slithered about on the icy stream.

Bernardo glided up. 'How are you getting on, ladies?' he said. Bernardo was the only one of the guinea pigs who could skate properly. 'I expect you're wondering why I'm so good,' he said.

'No, we're not,' Coco said. She was getting bored with Bernardo. He was a dreadful show-off.

'It is because I come from Peru,' Bernardo told her anyway. 'All Agoutis are brilliant at winter sports. But I, Bernardo Felipe Juan Carlos José Marino Ronaldo del Monte, am the best.' He did a quick triple axel and skated off again.

'How's it going, Co?' Terry whizzed up. Although he and the rest

of Banoffee's kids
had never tried
skating before, to
Coco's irritation
they seemed to have got the hang
of it quite quickly, even without
skating boots. So,
 annoyingly, had
Fuzzy. And Olaf the
Viking. *And* all the
other animals who had come
to the soup kitchen (apart from Alan,
who had wandered off in search
of more food). The squirrels and
the mice and the rabbits looked

as if they had been born to skate compared to her (especially the rabbits, because they had huge feet). In fact, far from being the best, Coco

reflected bitterly, she and Banoffee were the worst!

'Don't worry, Coco, your friends Rufus and Renarta will sort you out!' Fuzzy did a neat little spin and zoomed off.

'Yes, indeed we will!' a deep voice said.

Coco looked up. Thank goodness,

she thought, they're here. Two enormous hares were standing by the edge of the stream. Rufus and Renarta had finally arrived!

'You go, Coco,' Banoffee said. 'I'll join you in a minute. I need to straighten my knickers.'

Coco wobbled off. 'Cooee!' she called. 'I'm Coco!' She slid her way towards them on her tummy. The two hares waited for her. She picked herself up and looked at them brightly. At last she would learn to skate like the celebrities on *The Ice Factor*! She blinked. Rufus and Renarta weren't quite what

she'd been expecting. She'd never seen
a hare before, but she didn't realize
they were quite so big or had such
long pointy noses. 'Which one of you
is Rufus and which one is Renarta?'
she asked. The two hares looked very
similar.

'Er . . . he is,' Rufus and Renarta
said together, pointing at one another.

Coco frowned.

'I mean, er . . . she is,' Rufus and
Renarta both said.

Coco looked at the two animals
more closely. She had an uneasy
feeling something funny was going
on. Rufus and Renarta were wearing
onesies, like Alan's, except they were
hare onesies with long droopy ears and
great big back feet. But why would
a hare be wearing a hare onesie? It
didn't make any sense. Unless . . .

Coco backed away. Suddenly she
understood! She had been tricked
again. Rufus and Renarta weren't

really hares at all! They were foxes. They had gone on the Internet pretending to be hares so that they could catch her. And this time there was no Eduardo to rescue her.

'Recognize me now?' Renard said. He pulled back the head of his costume to reveal his foxy face. 'When will you learn that you should never talk to people you don't know on the Internet?' he sighed.

'Or invite strangers to parties?' the other fox added.

'But I thought you were Fuzzy's friends!' Coco squealed.

'You should be more careful about who you accept as a friend on the computer,' Renard said.

'Talking of friends, this is Thaddeus, my pal from the railway line. He's staying with me for the winter. He brought me a little present. Would you like to see it?'

Coco shook her head. Her knees trembled. She couldn't move she was so frightened. And even if she could move, she would just fall over. There was no way of warning Fuzzy and the others except to cry out. They were all too busy enjoying themselves on the ice to notice she was in danger (except for Banoffee, who was still straightening her knickers). And if she cried out, the foxes would definitely eat her.

Renard reached into his onesie and pulled out an object with a plastic handle and a gleaming metal cylinder. Coco recognized it at once. Henrietta kept one in her bedroom. Coco had often admired it. 'A hairdryer!' she snorted, trying to sound brave and clever at the same time. 'What are you going to do with that? Blow-dry us to death?

'No.' Renard eyed her hungrily.

'We're going to drown you all. Then we're going to take you back to the burrow and have a feast.' And he pointed the hairdryer at the ice and began to melt it.

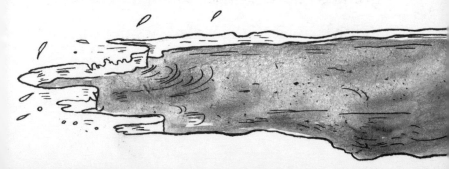

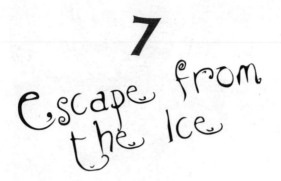

7
Escape from the Ice

Coco stared at the ice. As the blow-dryer warmed it, the white colour disappeared because the ice was turning into water. Coco looked behind her to all the animals skating and playing happily. 'Get off the ice!' she called. 'It's not safe! It's melting!'

The animals slowly stopped what they were doing. They skated towards Coco to see what was wrong.

'Not this way!' she called. She pointed at the ice between her and the bank of the stream. The blow-dryer had done its work. The ice had melted. The frozen section Coco was standing on jolted as it came away from the bank. Coco felt very scared but she tried not to show it. 'Quick! Go to the other bank!' she shouted.

The animals turned and made their way to the far bank. Banoffee stood on the bank, waiting to help her children off the ice. Suddenly a big paw pushed her aside and she fell over. The paw belonged to Thaddeus. He laughed.

'Not so fast, old lady. I've got work to do here.'

'Help, help!' cried Banoffee.

Thaddeus had *another* hairdryer in his hand.

'He's melting the ice on the other side of the stream,' Fuzzy shouted.

'We're trapped!' Bernardo cried.

Benjy, Banoffee's third-youngest child, reached the edge of the ice.

'Mum! Help me!' he called out to Banoffee, holding out his paw.

Banoffee struggled to her feet. 'I can't reach you!' she called out.

'Good!' said Thaddeus.

The ice on the far bank was melting. There was a pool of water between Benjy and his mum. He hadn't started swimming lessons yet. Holding on tight to her knickers, Banoffee leaped on to the ice to try and save him. Coco put her paws to her face. *The Ice Factor* was turning into a major wildlife disaster, and it was all her fault!

Suddenly Coco heard a noise above the cries of the animals. It sounded like an engine. She looked at the bushes behind

Renard, beyond the stream. The sound was coming from there. Seconds later, a vehicle charged through a small gap in the leaves and branches. Clumps of snow fell to the ground as the foliage moved. Coco didn't recognize the vehicle at first. But then she looked a bit closer and realized it was the truck with a ruler tied to the front of it!

Renard heard the sound and turned round. The truck was heading towards him. As it got close Coco saw that Eduardo was at the wheel, with Pepper and Blossom sitting next to him. She had never been so pleased to see anyone in her life.

'It's Renard!' she shouted to Eduardo. 'He's melting the ice with a hairdryer!'

'The fiend!' Eduardo drove the truck straight at Renard. The fox dropped his hairdryer and tried to escape to the side but it was too late.

The ruler bashed into Renard and pushed him towards the stream. Then, with one last nudge, it pushed him right into the water.

SPLASH!

'HOORAY!' All the animals cheered.

Renard paddled around in the freezing water, trying to remember how to swim.

'That'll teach you not to steal our food!' Eduardo called out to the fox.

'I haven't stolen anything. I haven't got any food! Otherwise why would I want to eat *you*?' spluttered Renard.

'You always want to eat us, even when you're not hungry,' Fuzzy pointed out.

'*I* don't want to eat you, I'm a vegetarian,' said Thaddeus from the other bank.

'So how come you were helping Renard melt the ice?' asked Terry.

'I was just being helpful to my friend.'

'Well, you're not being very helpful now,' Renard complained.

He was splashing around in the water. Reluctantly Thaddeus put down his blow-dryer and jumped into the freezing stream. He swam under the ice and came up on the other side, pushed Renard up out of the water on to the bank and then climbed out himself. The two foxes shook their coats and then sloped off to the burrow. They had enough hunting for one day.

Meanwhile, Pepper and Blossom jumped down from the cab and ran around to the front of the truck. They untied the ruler and laid it across the water, making a bridge for the animals to cross from the ice to the bank.

'That is clever,' said Coco as she held out her hand to help Benjy on to the ruler.

'It is not just clever, it is brilliant – and it was my idea!' said Eduardo.

'Well done,' said Coco to Eduardo, 'and well done to Pepper and Blossom for helping you.'

'Thanks,' said Pepper and Blossom together.

One by one Coco helped the animals off the ice. Once the animals reached the bank, Banoffee and Eduardo dried them off with the hairdryer Thaddeus had dropped.

Soon all of Banoffee's kids, Fuzzy, Olaf, Bernardo and all the squirrels and mice and rabbits were safely on the bank. Coco was the last to cross over and Banoffee helped her up.

'I'm hungry,' said Benjy.

'So am I,' said Blossom.

'It's teatime,' said Banoffee.

The animals set off back towards Banoffee's hutch for some more food.

'Halt!' Eduardo cried when they were a little further upstream.

A man was crouching at the edge of the ice.

'Why are we stopping?' asked Benjy.

'Shhh!' whispered Eduardo. 'There is an unknown human ahead.'

The man was holding a mobile phone at arm's length in front of him with one hand and a twig with a bit of wire on the end of it with the other.

'What's he doing?' asked Coco.

'He's fishing,' answered Fuzzy.

'But why is he talking to himself on the phone?' asked Coco.

'He's filming himself fishing,' answered Fuzzy.

All the animals fell silent and listened to what the man was saying.

'Here in Norway there are many

varieties of fish in the frozen fjords. So
I've cut a hole in the ice and I hope,
in a few minutes, a salmon will come
along and I can catch it for my dinner.
Meanwhile, I need to look out for any
polar bears that might want to catch
me for *their* dinner!'

He laughed to himself and looked around. The little animals shrank back into the bushes so they couldn't be seen.

'While I'm waiting, I'll treat myself to one of the walrus-dung cookies I baked earlier.'

The man reached into his pocket and brought out a cookie.

'That's not a walrus-dung cookie,' said Fuzzy. 'That's one of the special oat cookies that Ben baked for the animals and Henrietta left out for them!'

Eduardo scratched his head. 'You're right, *Señor* Fuzzy. That man is not eating no walrus-dung cookie. That man is not fishing no salmon. That man is not in no Norway.'

'You need some English lessons, cousin,' said Bernardo.

'No. What I need is a policeman.'

'Why? Is he breaking the law?' asked Coco.

'It's not just the law he is breaking, *señorita*. He is breaking my heart!' declared Eduardo. 'He is a crook.'

'A crook?' asked Olaf. 'Did he steal our food?'

'Yes, he did. And he is pretending to be in Norway when he is in the copse in Strawberry Park.'

'Why?' asked Coco. 'Why would he do that?'

'Because he is a liar and a thief and his name is Butch Grizzly.'

8

Saving Señor Eduardo

'Butch Grizzly!' Coco gasped.
'You mean the guy from the survival
programme?'

Eduardo nodded grimly. 'Butch
Baby, more like!' he grumbled.

'So it's all a hoax?' Terry asked.

Just then Alan wandered past in

his squirrel onesie. He made his way towards Butch Grizzly.

'Pssst!' Eduardo tried to get Alan's attention. '*Amigo!* Over here!'

Alan ignored him.

'Alan's still on the lookout for something to eat!' Fuzzy reminded Eduardo. 'He thinks Butch Grizzly really *is* going to catch a fish.'

Alan sauntered towards the stream. 'Miaow!' he said hopefully.

Butch Grizzly looked up. For a few seconds he stared at Alan in surprise. Then his face twisted into a look of pure terror.

'What's the matter with him?' Coco said. 'Is he afraid of cats?' She didn't see how anyone could be afraid of Alan. Even mice weren't scared of Alan, he was so lazy.

'I don't think so, Co,' Terry said.
'It's all fake, remember? He's just
pretending.'

The guinea pigs watched to see
what would happen next.

'Just as I feared!' Butch Grizzly
gasped. 'A polar bear!'

'Where?' Banoffee looked around.
'I can't see a polar bear.'

'He means Alan, Mum,' Terry explained. 'Butch Grizzly is pretending that Alan is a polar bear to make it seem as if he's really in danger. It's to trick all the people watching his show on TV.'

'That cheat will stop at nothing!' Eduardo fumed.

Coco and Fuzzy exchanged glances. They had never seen Eduardo look so steamed up, even when he ate the chilli in Fuzzy's Volcano Veg.

'It's coming closer!' Butch Grizzly jerked his phone about as Alan closed in.

'Now what's he doing?' Banoffee asked.

'He's still filming,' Terry said. 'He's trying to make it look as if he's running away from the polar bear.'

Suddenly Butch Grizzly went rigid. He held the phone inches in front of his face, so that the TV audience couldn't see Alan. 'It's only a few metres away now,' he hissed. 'And I can tell you, it's huge!'

'Alan's not that fat,' Banoffee commented.

'He's *pretending*!' her children chorused.

'Oh yes,' Banoffee said. 'I forgot.' She pulled her knickers up. 'I must say he's very good at it, isn't he? I might start watching his show.'

Coco shook her head. Banoffee really wasn't very bright.

'Aaarrrggghhhh! It's got me!' Butch Grizzly dropped the phone face down on the snow. Then he grabbed Alan around the tummy and lifted him into the air.

The guinea pigs looked on. 'He's not going to hurt Alan, is he?' Coco said.

'I don't think so,' Fuzzy replied. 'He's just trying to make it sound more realistic on the film.'

'Take that!' Butch Grizzly lumped
Alan to and fro, stamping and scuffing
at the snow with his big boots.

Alan didn't seem to mind very
much. He picked at Butch Grizzly's
beard with his front paws.

'Alan's fighting back!' Banoffee punched the air. 'Go, Alan!'

'No, he's not, Banoffee,' Coco said. 'He's after the cookie crumbs in Butch Grizzly's beard.'

'Arrrrgggghhhh!' Butch Grizzly yelled. He held Alan at arm's length. 'There's only one thing for it,' he shouted. 'I'll have to play dead!' He put Alan down and lay flat on the ground beside the upturned phone, wheezing heavily.

Alan gave his pockets one last sniff and ambled off.

'Phew!' Butch Grizzly hissed. 'It's leaving. I'll give it a few more minutes to be sure.' Quietly he got to his feet, leaving the phone face down on the snow. He took out a penknife from his pocket and used it to rip holes in his jacket. Then he grabbed a handful of mud from the bank of the stream and rubbed it all over his face and beard.

'He's making it look as though he really *was* attacked!' Coco exclaimed. 'What a fake!'

Butch Grizzly snatched up the phone. 'That was close,' he panted, aiming the camera at his dirty face and torn jacket. 'But that's what it takes to survive in the wilderness. Guts.'

He jutted out his chin. 'Now, back to salmon fishing.' He picked up the twig.

'I can't take no more of this!' Eduardo stormed. He took off his satchel and held it out to Fuzzy. 'Hold this.'

Fuzzy took it. 'What are you going to do?'

'I'm going to show Butch Baby who's really got guts in this neighbourhood.' Eduardo marched off in the direction of the stream.

'Can *we* come?' asked Blossom and Pepper.

'Not this time,' Eduardo shouted.

'Something tells me this isn't a good idea,' Fuzzy muttered.

'Don't worry, friend!' Bernardo clapped a paw on his shoulder. 'Butch Grizzly will not harm Eduardo. He did not harm Alan, after all.'

'That's probably because he thought Alan was a polar bear,' Banoffee remarked.

'Mum, give up, would you?' Terry said.

Eduardo scampered up to Butch Grizzly and wriggled into the top of his boot. This time Butch Grizzly's face registered genuine shock. He looked down. A large black-and-silver guinea pig was burrowing into his sock.

'Ouch!' he cried in a shrill voice.

'Eduardo must have bitten him!' Coco whispered.

'Oh dear,' Fuzzy said.

'Not so butch now, are you, Baby?!' Eduardo shouted. The animals understood him, but all Butch Grizzly heard was an angry *chutter chutter chutter*. 'I'll be back in a minute,' he told his audience. He pressed a button on his phone.

'He's stopped recording,' Terry said.

'Oh dear,' Fuzzy said again.

Butch Grizzly's big hairy hand reached down and grabbed Eduardo. He hauled the guinea pig out of his sock and dangled it in front of him.

'A guinea pig,' he said. He scratched his beard with his free hand. 'Hmmm . . .' Then he took off his hat, put Eduardo inside it and tied it up by the earflaps.

The animals watched in horror.

'Oh dear!' said Fuzzy for a third time.

'Fuzzy, stop saying "Oh dear" and do something, can't you?' Coco cried. 'He's captured Eduardo! He can't get out.'

'I'm thinking!' Fuzzy said. And he *was* thinking. He was thinking that Butch Grizzly wasn't pretending any more. He looked like he meant business.

Butch Grizzly had switched his phone back on. 'When I said "ow" just now' – he grinned at the camera –

'what I meant was . . . er . . . 'ow's that for a piece of luck . . . ?'

'What's he talking about?' Banoffee demanded. 'It's not very lucky having a guinea pig bite your ankle. Especially when it's got teeth like Eduardo's.'

'He's pretending again, Mum,' Terry sighed. 'Listen.'

The animals paid rapt attention.

'. . . because something interesting just landed in one of my traps,' Butch Grizzly went on. 'It's a . . . er . . . Norwegian lemming – absolutely delicious to eat roasted with nut stuffing. In a minute I'll show you how

to prepare it, but first let's get the
fire going.' He got up and started
collecting twigs.

'He's still pretending, right?'
Banoffee said.

'No, Mum, I don't think he is this
time,' Terry said quietly. 'Maybe you
should get the little ones home.'

'All right,' Banoffee agreed.
'Come on, kids, let's go. If we're quick
we can watch the rest of it on TV!'
She gathered up the smallest of her
children and trotted off.

Coco waited until she was out
of earshot. 'Oh, Fuzzy, what are we

going to do?' she sniffed. 'He's going to
cook Eduardo!'

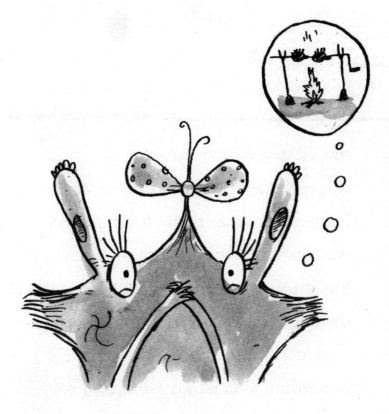

9

Hot Pants

Butch Grizzly knelt down, cleared away some snow with his hands and put the twigs he'd collected in a pile on the bare ground in front of him. He arranged them in a pyramid shape, reached into his pocket and took out a lighter. He flicked the switch and a flame appeared.

He lowered the flame to the twigs and the small, dry ones took light. They burned orange.

Fuzzy, Coco, Terry, Olaf and Bernardo were all transfixed, It was as if they'd been hypnotized by the sight of the flame.

Coco was the first to snap out of it. 'Quick, everyone!' she said. 'Think of what we can do to save Eduardo!'

The sight of the flame reminded Fuzzy of cooking. He thought of his favourite recipes and the fun he'd had making them. He thought of frying onions and stirring soup. He thought of whipping eggs and melting

marshmallows. And then
he thought of . . .

'Hairdryers!'

He had once used a hairdryer to melt
marshmallows and turn the edges brown.

'What use are they?' said Coco.

'We can use them to burn Butch
Grizzly's trousers.'

Fuzzy, Bernardo, Olaf and Terry dashed to get the hairdryers which had been left on the ground after the foxes ran away. Fuzzy and Bernardo dragged one of them towards Butch Grizzly. Olaf and Terry dragged the other.

The fire was burning brightly now. It was nice and hot. Butch Grizzly grabbed his hat. He carefully undid the ties and reached into it to pull Eduardo out.

'Mmm, delicious,' he said to the camera.

The guinea pigs crept forward. They placed the hairdryers just behind Butch

Grizzly. Fuzzy raised his paw. He remembered the battles he'd seen in the war films he watched with Ben on Sunday afternoons. He copied what the generals said when they were telling the troops to shoot the cannons.

'Ready . . . ?'

Bernardo, Olaf and Terry nodded that they were ready.

'Aim . . . !'

The guinea pigs positioned the hairdryers so that they were pointing right at Butch Grizzly's bottom.

'Fire!'

The guinea pigs switched on the hairdryers.

'Turn it to MAX,' shouted Terry.

Intense heat burned into Butch Grizzly's trousers.

'OOOOOOOWWWWWWW!'

Butch Grizzly leaped in the air. He dropped the phone. He dropped Eduardo. He clutched his bottom with both hands.

Eduardo ran to his friends and all the guinea pigs scampered away as fast as they could. They didn't want Butch Grizzly to see *them*, but they *did* want to see what happened to *him*.

Butch Grizzly clutched his trousers and rubbed his bottom. He hopped from one foot to another like a crazy kangaroo. The guinea pigs squeaked happily.

'Are you OK?' Bernardo whispered to Eduardo.

'Yes, cousin. Thank you for saving me.'

'It wasn't me, it was all of us.'

The guinea pigs stopped squeaking when they saw two people walk up to Butch Grizzly.

'Hand over the guinea pig!' said a voice that Fuzzy recognized.

It was Henrietta!

'I haven't got a guinea pig,' Butch Grizzly replied.

'You've eaten it!' cried another voice that Fuzzy recognized.

It was Ben!

'I haven't! It ran away!' replied Butch Grizzly.

'Just a minute, I recognize you,' interrupted Henrietta. 'You're Butch Grizzly, the TV adventurer. Isn't he, Ben?'

'Yes, yes, he is. But aren't you meant to be in Norway? This is Strawberry Park. Norway is about a thousand kilometres away,' said Ben.

'Thanks,' said Butch Grizzly. 'I'll be off then.'

'No, you won't,' said Henrietta, 'not before you've talked to the police.'

'I don't need to talk to the police. I've done nothing wrong. I'm just lost,' said Butch Grizzly.

'You're not lost, you're a thief,' said Henrietta.

'I haven't stolen anything.'

'Yes, you have. Put your hand in your pocket and show me what you have in there.'

'With pleasure. It's just a few broken biscuits.'

Butch Grizzly did as Henrietta had asked. He held out his hand.

Ben burst into tears. 'Those are not just any old broken biscuits,' he sobbed. 'Those are my home-baked oat cookies that I made for the starving animals in this frozen copse. And you stole them.'

Fuzzy raised his paws to applaud Ben's speech, but then he realized it would make too much noise and dropped them back to his sides. He didn't want Ben and Henrietta to see him outside. They didn't know that Fuzzy and Coco could let themselves in and out of their hutch. They probably thought their beloved pets were curled up in their soft bed of hay, sound asleep.

Just then a bright light shone in Butch Grizzly's face. It came from a policeman's torch.

'You're under arrest,' the policeman said.

The policeman took Butch Grizzly away. Ben and Henrietta made their way back to the house.

Fuzzy looked around proudly at his guinea-pig friends. It was time to go home. Just then he realized someone was missing.

'Where's Coco?' he said.

10
Best Friends Forever

Later that evening, when Butch Grizzly
was being interviewed at the police station
and Ben and Henrietta were reading
each other bedtime stories, the campfire
was still burning in the copse. Around it
sat Fuzzy, Eduardo, Bernardo, Olaf, Terry
and Coco. Banoffee was babysitting her

little children in the warmth of her owner's house while the guinea pigs outside were kept warm by the glowing campfire. Whenever it showed signs of dying down they took it in turns to feed it with twigs. All the boys were looking at Coco as if she were a celebrity.

'So how did you tell Ben and Henrietta that Butch Grizzly was trying to cook Eduardo in the copse?' asked Fuzzy.

'I posted a message on the Animal News Feed,' said Coco. 'I've heard Ben and Henrietta talk about it. They both follow it because they love animals, and when they saw that a guinea pig was in danger they came straight down here.'

'That was clever of you, Co,' said Terry. 'You're becoming a real whizz on the computer. Soon you'll be teaching me!'

'Not really. It was my fault Rufus and Renarta came to the ice-skating competition.'

'No, it wasn't,' said Fuzzy. 'I need to be more careful who I accept as friends on Micespace.'

'You're all better than me,' said Olaf. 'I can't even work out which machine is the computer. I look through the windows of the houses

around the copse and I can't tell the difference between the computer, the television and the fridge.'

'The last one is easy,' said Fuzzy. 'The fridge is always the one with the food in.'

'Don't talk about food – it's making me hungry,' said Coco.

'Then it must be time for supper,' said Fuzzy.

'Supper?' said Bernardo.

'But we still have no food in this copse,' said Eduardo.

'We do,' said Fuzzy. 'Ben and Henrietta left more cookies for the animals. And this time they won't be stolen!' He handed some cookie chunks to his friends.

While the guinea pigs tucked in, Bernardo took his guitar from his back and started to strum. Eduardo hummed a tune.

'May I sing along?' asked Bernardo.

'Of course,' said Eduardo, and together they sang:

> *'We're Agoutis, my beauties,*
> *Los mountains are our home,*
> *Our peoples live in freedom,*
> *Among the grass we roams.'*

The two guinea pigs sang lovely harmonies. Coco watched them with bright eyes. They were both so handsome and so talented.

> 'We came to Strawberry Park,
> And saw you live in hutches,
> We wanted then to free you,
> From the humans' clutches.
>
> But now we see you love
> Their food and warmth and kisses,
> And you can also join us
> Out here if you so wishes.

So under the starry sky,
We can be together,
No need for competition,
Cos we're best friends forever.'

'That's lovely,' Coco said. 'You should go in for a TV talent show.'

'NO!' said Eduardo, Bernardo, Fuzzy, Terry and Olaf.

'We've had enough of talent shows,' said Fuzzy.

'You're right. We have,' said Coco. 'Real life is much more fun.'

'Much, much more fun,' said Eduardo.

They all looked into the flames. There was a contented silence which was broken by Coco.

'Although I'd like to get back for *The Ice Factor* results.'

'You can watch them later on the laptop,' said Terry.

'Then can I have an online chat with my mum?' asked Eduardo.

'And can I order a new guitar string?' asked Bernardo.

'OK,' said Fuzzy. 'What about you, Olaf? Anything you'd like to do on the computer?'

'I'd like to learn how to turn it on,' said Olaf.

'Wow!' said Coco. 'Looks like we're all going to be guinea pigs online.'

The End

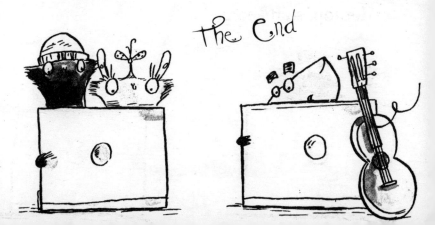

Draw Alan!

Alan loves attention, which is why he wants you to draw him.

Can you fill in the gaps of the picture on the left, by copying the picture on the right?

Then, you can colour him in! What colour do you think his squirrel onesie should be?

Olaf's Very Viking Word Search

Olaf needs help with this puzzle. Can you help him find the words in the list in the grid below? The words can be vertical, horizontal or diagonal.

N	O	R	W	A	Y	Q	T
C	B	P	M	T	J	J	D
O	X	O	F	Z	W	T	V
R	Q	L	Z	I	A	A	I
D	G	A	B	O	S	V	K
A	G	R	B	M	F	H	I
I	D	U	Z	R	X	A	N
G	R	I	Z	Z	L	Y	G

VIKING

NORWAY

BOAT

GRIZZLY

POLAR

FISH

Coco's EVEN HARDER Word Search

Coco thinks she's brilliant at everything, but sometimes even she needs help. Can you help her with this very tough puzzle?

First, you fill in the blank. Then, you have to find the word in the grid below. And, after all that work, you should have a snooze.

1. Fuzzy's favourite TV show is called _ _ _ _ _ _ Warmers
2. The guinea pigs live in _ _ _ _ _ berry Park
3. Renard pretends to be a _ _ _ _ so he can join in the ice-skating
4. Bernardo plays the _ _ _ _ _ _
5. Fuzzy puts too much _ _ _ _ _ _ _ in Eduardo's food
6. Coco loves The _ _ _ Factor

S	W	B	C	U	T	D	W
T	I	C	L	X	G	B	P
R	N	C	Q	N	U	Z	V
A	T	H	O	A	I	S	C
W	E	I	U	P	T	O	N
G	R	L	C	H	A	R	E
P	G	L	Y	E	R	H	T
S	A	I	W	G	C	J	M

READ ALL THE BOOKS IN THIS HAY-LARIOUS SERIES!

THEN YOU'LL REALLY REALLY LOVE THE BRAND-NEW SERIES

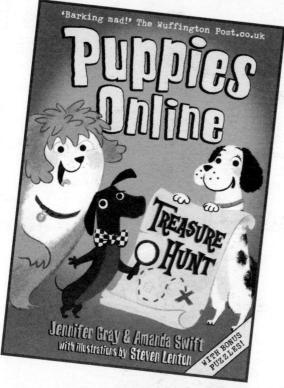

WOOFING IN A SHOP NEAR YOU FROM AUGUST 2014

For special offers,
chapter samplers,
competitions
and more,
visit . . .

www.quercusbooks.co.uk
♥ @quercuskids